W9-ARJ-266

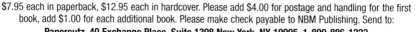

NANCY DREW

#17 DREW

girl detective ®

Night of the Living Chatchke

STEFAN PETRUCHA & SARAH KINNEY • Writers
SHO MURASE • Artist
with 3D CG elements and color by CARLOS JOSE GUZMAN
Based on the series by
CAROLYN KEENE

PAPERCUTZ™

New York

Night of the Living Chatchke
STEFAN PETRUCHA & SARAH KINNEY – Writers
SHO MURASE – Artist
with 3D CG elements and color by CARLOS JOSE GUZMAN
BRYAN SENKA – Letterer
MIKHAELA REID and MASHEKA WOOD – Production
MICHAEL PETRANEK - Editorial Assistant
JIM SALICRUP
Editor-in-Chief

ISBN 10: 1-59707-143-9 paperback edition
ISBN 13: 978-1-59707-143-7 paperback edition
ISBN 10: 1-59707-144-7 hardcover edition
ISBN 13: 978-1-59707-144-4 hardcover edition

Printed in China.
February 2009 by WKT Co. LTD.
3/F Phase I Leader Industrial Centre
188 Texaco Road, Tsuen Wan, N.T.
Hong Kong

Distributed by Macmillan.

10   9   8   7   6   5   4   3   2   1

NANCY DREW, GIRL DETECTIVE HERE. WHEN LAWYER-DAD **CARSON DREW** ASKED ME ALONG TO ISTANBUL, TURKEY, HOW COULD I SAY NO?

HE WAS HERE TO OVERSEE THE SALE OF AN ANCESTRAL ESTATE BELONGING TO A CLIENT, **ALDA OKTAR**. MEANWHILE, THE THREE OF US TOOK IN THE SIGHTS, LIKE THIS PLACE, THE **GRAND BAZAAR**.

THE *KAPALI CARSI*, OR COVERED MARKET, HAS **MILES** OF PASSAGEWAYS AND OVER **4000 SHOPS**! YOU'D THINK I'D HAVE **LOTS** TO LOOK AT, BUT I COULDN'T HELP BUT BE **FASCINATED** BY THE WAY MY DAD WAS STARING AT ALDA.

I THINK HE **LIKED** HER.

CHAPTER ONE: THE QUITE BIZARRE BAZAAR

JUST AS I WAS WISHING I WAS ONE OF THOSE DAUGHTERS WHO WEARS AN IPOD CRANKED UP LOUD...

...WE ARRIVED AT ALDA'S HOME.

TURKEY WAS ONCE PART OF THE ROMAN EMPIRE AND *THAT* ARCHITECTURE IS CALLED *BYZANTINE*. THEN, IN THE 13TH CENTURY, CONQUERING TURKS STARTED BUILDING OTTOMAN ARCHITECTURE, SOME OF IT FIT FOR A SULTAN.

BEAUTIFUL, ISN'T IT? IT HAS BEEN IN MY FAMILY FOR CENTURIES.

BUT, THEN WHY ARE YOU *SELLING* IT?

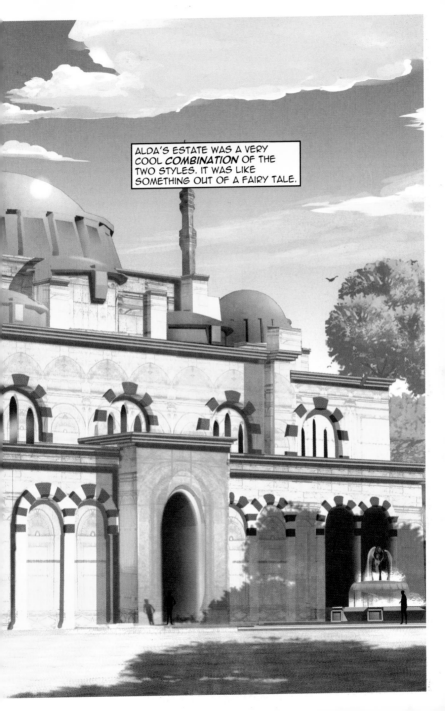

ALDA'S ESTATE WAS A VERY *COOL* **COMBINATION** OF THE TWO STYLES. IT WAS LIKE SOMETHING OUT OF A FAIRY TALE.

WE'LL GET THIS ALL SORTED OUT, I PROMISE.

YOUR MONEY TROUBLES WILL BE OVER SOON. *HARLAND SEVERINO* HAS MADE A VERY *GENEROUS* BID.

OF COURSE! *HE'S* BEEN DYING TO BUY IT FOR YEARS.

I REALIZE WE CAN'T *REALLY* PUT A PRICE ON YOUR ANCESTRAL HOME.

THIS MUST BE VERY PAINFUL.

MY DAD WAS PRETTY SENSITIVE TO ALDA'S SITUATION, BUT *I* WAS SENSING SHE MISSED THAT PLAQUE EVEN *MORE* THAN SHE WAS GOING TO MISS THE HOUSE.

...RIGHT *HERE*?!

I'VE BEEN LOOKING FOR SOMETHING TO COVER THAT UGLY *CRACK*. IT'S THE PERFECT THING, DON'T YOU THINK?

OH, YES, IT'S THE... *THING*, ALL RIGHT.

YOU KNOW, THE SELLER SAID THAT STATUE'S *HAUNTED*!

HA! HA! HA!

I THOUGHT MAYBE IF I **UNDERSTOOD** THE STATUE, I'D APPRECIATE IT MORE, BUT I COULDN'T FIND ANYTHING **LIKE** IT IN ANY BOOKS.

FRANKLY, I WAS A LITTLE BORED. THE ONLY MYSTERY FOR ME TO THINK ABOUT WAS THAT THERE REALLY WAS NO ACCOUNTING FOR TASTE.

BUT IT HAD BEEN A **LONG** DAY, SO...

HMPH! NOTHING.

JUST *YOU,* MOCKING ME.

HUH.

I KNOW THAT THE POWER OF SUGGESTION IS PRETTY... WELL, *POWERFUL*.

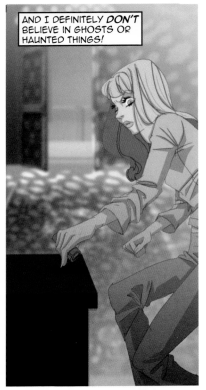

AND I DEFINITELY *DON'T* BELIEVE IN GHOSTS OR HAUNTED THINGS!

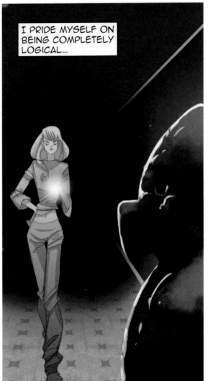

I PRIDE MYSELF ON BEING COMPLETELY LOGICAL...

...CONSIDERING ONLY THE *FACTS* IN ANY GIVEN SITUATION.

I KNOW THERE ARE *SOME* THINGS IN THIS WORLD THAT *SEEM UN*EXPLAINABLE.

BUT, GENERALLY, THEY'RE *NOT!*

NANCY?!

NOW I'VE GOT--

--YOU?!

THAT MORNING, THE PLOT *THICKENED*. ALDA DISCOVERED SOME SMALL *HEIRLOOMS* WERE MISSING.

IT WAS TIME TO TELL SOMEONE ABOUT THE *STATUE*. GIVEN HOW UPSET ALDA WAS, I THOUGHT I'D BETTER START WITH MY DAD.

BUT, IT SEEMS *HE* HAD SOMETHING PRIVATE TO DISCUSS WITH *ME*!

TURNS OUT IT WAS THE *SAME* SOMETHING... SORT OF.

NANCY, I'M SORRY TO ASK THIS, BUT I *KNOW* YOU DON'T LIKE THAT STATUE AND I *KNOW* YOUR FRIENDS THOUGHT YOU SHOULD MAKE ALDA THINK IT WAS HAUNTED...

BUT, I ALSO KNOW *YOU* WOULDN'T... COULDN'T *POSSIBLY* INDULGE IN SUCH NONSENSE... *WOULD* YOU?!

DAD! HOW COULD YOU EVEN *ASK*? OF *COURSE* NOT!

BUT WE *MIGHT* HAVE BEEN TALKING ABOUT THAT WHEN YOUR DAD PICKED UP YOUR PHONE --

WHICH YOU *DROPPED*, NANCY!

METHINKS THE LACK OF SLEEP IS AFFECTING SOMEONE'S DETECTING, GIRL!

RIGHT. PERFECT!

THE PROBLEM IS, NOW DAD WON'T KNOW WHETHER TO BELIEVE ME OR NOT IF I *DO* TELL HIM THERE'S SOMETHING WEIRD ABOUT THAT UGLY STATUE!

OUR SIGHTSEEING THAT DAY WAS A LITTLE MORE ON THE SERIOUS SIDE. IT STARTED AT *POLICE HEADQUARTERS*, WHERE ALDA'S SERVANT, RASHIK, WAS BEING HELD.

DAD HAD FINALLY ARRANGED FOR THE RELEASE OF THE *PLAQUE* RASHIK HAD BEEN CAUGHT WITH.

ALDA, MEANWHILE, HAD ASKED TO MEET WITH THE FORMERLY FAITHFUL RASHIK. HIS FAMILY HAD SERVED HER FAMILY FOR AS FAR BACK AS ANYONE COULD REMEMBER, AND SHE NEEDED TO UNDERSTAND WHAT HAPPENED.

WHILE DAD FILLED OUT THE PAPERWORK, ALDA ASKED ME TO SIT IN ON HER VISIT WITH RASHIK.

I WAS SURPRISED TO HEAR SHE STILL HADN'T PRESSED CHARGES AND SEEMED *CONFUSED* ABOUT WHAT TO DO.

ALDA HOPED TO GET A CLUE FROM RASHIK. BUT EVEN NOW, THE STRANGELY *EXPRESSIONLESS* MAN HAD SAID *NOTHING* IN HIS OWN DEFENSE.

RASHIK, I JUST DON'T UNDERSTAND... HOW *COULD* YOU..?

PLEASE JUST *TELL* ME *WHY* YOU STOLE THE PLAQUE?!

AFFECTION FOR SOMEONE YOU'VE LIVED WITH ALL YOUR LIFE IS ONLY NATURAL...

...BUT YOU DIDN'T HAVE TO BE A DETECTIVE TO SENSE SOMETHING MORE... SOME *DEEPER* EMOTION BETWEEN THEM.

WHILE ALDA TRIED TO SOLVE HER MYSTERY, I SET OFF TO GET SOME *ANSWERS* OF MY OWN.

STARTING WITH FINDING THE *OLD MAN* WHO SOLD MY DAD THE STATUE IN THE FIRST PLACE.

BUT, *NO ONE* SEEMED TO KNOW THE LITTLE MAN WITH THE BEARD AND THE UGLY STATUE.

AFTER WALKING AROUND FOR AN HOUR OR MORE, I FOUND MYSELF STANDING AT WHAT I WAS SURE WAS THE *EXACT SPOT* WHERE WE'D BOUGHT THE STATUE.

ONLY, EVERYTHING WAS GONE.

NOT EVERYTHING. APPARENTLY THE OLD MAN LEFT IN A *HURRY* -- LIKE A CARTOON CHARACTER, HE'D RACED OFF LEAVING HIS *BEARD* BEHIND.

BUT NOT BEFORE HE'D BLOWN A *MONSTER* BUBBLE. THE BEARD WAS *COVERED* WITH CHEWING GUM.

SOMEHOW, I IMAGINED AN OLD STREET VENDOR BEING MORE INTO CHEWING *TOBACCO* THAN GUM.

WELL, AT LEAST *SOMETHING* IS BACK TO NORMAL!

I'D HOPED SHE'D SMILE, BUT IT WAS PRETTY CLEAR ALDA WAS STILL FEELING ANYTHING *BUT* NORMAL, AND FINDING LITTLE COMFORT IN THAT COLD BRASS PLAQUE.

I JUST DON'T KNOW WHAT I WOULD DO WITHOUT YOU AND NANCY HERE, CARSON.

I'M JUST *SO* GRATEFUL!

THAT NIGHT I KEPT WONDERING, WHAT *WOULD* ALDA DO IF WE WEREN'T HERE? SHE SEEMED SO SAD IT COULDN'T JUST BE THE HOUSE, NOT EVEN A HOUSE AS GREAT AS *THIS.*

IT FELT LIKE ANOTHER PIECE IN A *BIG* PUZZLE.

OH, WELL. THE DARK QUIET CAN BE A GREAT TIME FOR CONNECTING PUZZLE PIECES IN YOUR HEAD.

ALDA'S SADNESS... THE BEARD... RASHIK... THE PLAQUE... THE STATUE... ALL FIT TOGETHER TO MAKE A STORY, BUT I COULDN'T QUITE GET --

THUMP
THUMP
THUMP

FOOT-STEPS?!

YEP. DEFINITELY FOOTSTEPS.

THUMP
THUMP
THUMP

÷GASP!÷

OKAY, *THIS* WAS FREAKY. THE STATUE WAS GONE!

MUCH AS I WOULD HAVE LIKED IT TO, I WAS STILL *PRETTY* SURE THE STATUE DIDN'T JUST GET UP AND WALK AWAY.

TH*U*MP
TH*U*MP
TH*U*MP

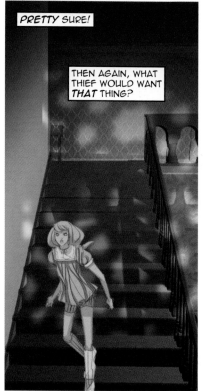

PRETTY SURE!

THEN AGAIN, WHAT THIEF WOULD WANT *THAT* THING?

GREAT. THESE STEPS GO TO THE BASEMENT. NO LIGHTS.

AND EACH BASEMENT SEEMED *OLDER* THAN THE LAST.

I STARTED TO FEEL LIKE I WAS...

...GOING BACKWARDS...

...THROUGH *TIME*.

IF THIS WAS *ANOTHER* WEIRD DREAM, I WAS STARTING TO MISS THE FIRST ONE WITH THE UGLY STATUE AND THE LOUSY DÉCOR!

AGAIN, NOT EXACTLY WHAT I WAS EXPECTING. INSTEAD OF GETTING A WHOLE PICTURE, I WAS ONLY GETTING MORE PUZZLE PIECES!

WHO WERE THESE GUYS? THEY CERTAINLY DIDN'T LOOK LIKE *PLUMBERS!* WHAT WERE THEY DIGGING FOR? AND WHY DID THEY HAVE *ALDA'S PLAQUE*???

FINALLY, WE HAVE YOU!

ONE OF THE MEN SPOKE ENGLISH. HE SOUNDED AMERICAN. STILL, I DIDN'T *UNDERSTAND*...

...WHAT DID HE MEAN BY '*FINALLY*'?

IT WAS *YOU* ALL ALONG! WASN'T IT? *CONFESS!*

HEY, YOU DEFINITELY AREN'T WEARING THE LATEST IN *HELPFUL CITIZEN* ATTIRE AND FRANKLY, I'M NOT BIG ON CONFESSING TO *CROOKS!*

=MOAN=

=MOAN=

AHHHHHH!

BUT, FORTUNATELY, SOMEONE ELSE *DID* CARE WHAT HAPPENED TO ME.

NANCY! ARE YOU OKAY?!

YOU WEREN'T IN YOUR *BED*, THE BASEMENT DOORS WERE *OPEN*, WE KEPT SEARCHING DEEPER AND *DEEPER*...

WHAT ARE YOU DOING DOWN *HERE*?!

SOLVING MYSTERIES! WELL, ONE OUT OF *TWO*, ANYWAY!

WELL, *THAT*... AND I LIKE HAWA'S FOOD BETTER THAN MY AUNT'S.

I'M SO SORRY, TOVIK! I KNOW YOU LOVE YOUR FATHER, BUT, IF RASHIK WERE *INNOCENT*, WHY WOULD HE REMAIN SILENT?

MY DAD *IS* INNOCENT! HE WAS *PROTECTING* THE PLAQUE, BECAUSE HE KNEW THOSE MEN WANTED TO STEAL IT!

AND TONIGHT, THEY *DID!*

SHE WAS UPSET WHEN *RASHIK*, A TRUSTED SERVANT, WAS CAUGHT STEALING A *PLAQUE*. TO CHEER HER UP, DAD BOUGHT HER THIS UGLY, SUPPOSEDLY *HAUNTED* STATUE.

WHY IS THERE A CITY UNDER THE BASEMENT? *WHAT* DO THOSE THIEVES WANT? THAT'S WHAT I PLAN TO FIND OUT.

IF I SURVIVE!

SEE WHAT I MEAN ABOUT THE DARK?

NANCY DREW, GIRL DETECTIVE, HERE TO TELL YOU THAT NO MATTER WHERE YOU GO, DARK IS *STILL* DARK.

AND NOT ONLY AM I CLIMBING DOWN A DEEP *DARK* HOLE, I'M TOTALLY IN THE *DARK* ABOUT A MAJOR MYSTERY.

SEE, I CAME TO TURKEY WITH MY DAD, CARSON, SO HE COULD HELP SELL *ALDA OKTAR'S* ANCESTRAL ESTATE.

IT *DID* GET AROUND, EVEN TO THE MANY SUB-BASEMENTS, WHERE I FOLLOWED AND LEARNED RASHIK'S SON *TOVIK* WAS HIDING INSIDE, HOPING TO CLEAR HIS DAD'S NAME.

HE'D FOLLOWED THREE *THIEVES* WHO'D TAKEN THAT *PLAQUE* AND USED IT TO OPEN A DOOR TO AN ENTIRE ANCIENT *CITY* BENEATH THE HOUSE!

DON'T MISS NANCY DREW GRAPHIC NOVEL #18 – "CITY UNDER THE BASEMENT"

WATCH OUT FOR PAPERCUTZ™

Welcome to the backpages of NANCY DREW Graphic Novel #17 "Night of the Living Chatchke." In case you're still wondering, a "chatchke," (or chatchka or tchotchke) is a knick-knack, or an inexpensive souvenir, or worthless piece of junk. See how educational a Papercutz graphic novel can be?

Around the same time we're sending NANCY DREW #17 to our printers (Happy Year of the Ox, printers!) we're also going back to press for the big eighth printing of the Girl Detective's comics debut --- NANCY DREW #1 "The Demon of River Heights." In fact, that graphic novel, along with THE HARDY BOYS graphic novel #1 "The Ocean of Osyria," published in early 2005 were the debut graphic novels from a little company called Papercutz (that's us!).

Since that historic premiere printing ND #1 has gone through all sorts of changes and minor tweaks. Perhaps the biggest was a few printings ago, when NANCY DREW artist Sho Murase decided to make some incredible changes to the color art. If you compare the latest printings to the first, you'll see that many pages have been virtually recolored, looking even more vibrant and dramatic than before. And here's the amazing part – Sho decided to make all these changes on her own. We were completely pleased with the earlier color work, but Sho the perfectionist wasn't, and she took it upon herself to give this graphic novel a gorgeous upgrade.

We're so happy to have Sho onboard as NANCY DREW's regular artist – she's done every cover, and every graphic novel except #5 and #7 – as she's captured that special essence that has made Nancy Drew America's favorite Girl Detective. Of course, we mustn't forget Stefan Petrucha, who has written every graphic novel based on Carolyn Keene's super-sleuth. Stefan's writer-wife Sarah Kinney has recently joined Stefan in creating scripts, and the stories and mysteries are getting even more exciting than ever before.

Papercutz publisher Terry Nantier and I (Jim Salicrup, editor-in-chief) are proud to report that thanks to our readers' loyal support, Papercutz is not only still producing four all-new NANCY DREW and four all-new HARDY BOYS graphic novels every year, but we're also publishing quite a few other titles you may love just as much as NANCY DREW. On the next few pages we talk a lot about CLASSICS ILLUSTRATED and CLASSICS ILLUSTRATED DELUXE, which we're sure you'll enjoy.

Now there's just enough room left to thank you! Yes, YOU! We greatly appreciate you're picking up this graphic novel, and hope you enjoyed it as much as we enjoyed putting it together. Let us know what you think, send your comments to me at salicrup@papercutz.com or by mail to Jim Salicrup, PAPERCUTZ, 40 Exchange Place, Ste 1308, New York, NY 10005. And be sure to check us out at www.papercutz.com for all the latest new developments!

Thanks,

Jim

CLASSICS Illustrated

Featuring Stories by the World's Greatest Authors

Returns in two new series from Papercutz!

The original, best-selling series of comics adaptations of the world's greatest literature, CLASSICS ILLUSTRATED, returns in two new formats--the original, featuring abridged adaptations of classic novels, and CLASSICS ILLUSTRATED DELUXE, featuring longer, more expansive adaptations-from graphic novel publisher Papercutz. "We're very proud to say that Papercutz has received such an enthusiastic reception from librarians and school teachers for its NANCY DREW and HARDY BOYS graphic novels as well as THE LIFE OF POPE JOHN PAUL II...*IN COMICS!*, that it only seemed logical for us to bring back the original CLASSICS ILLUSTRATED comicbook series beloved by parents, educators, and librarians," explained Papercutz Publisher, Terry Nantier. "We can't thank the enlightened librarians and teachers who have supported Papercutz enough. And we're thrilled that they're so excited about CLASSICS ILLUSTRATED."

Upcoming titles include The Invisible Man, Tales from the Brothers Grimm, and Through The Looking-Glass.

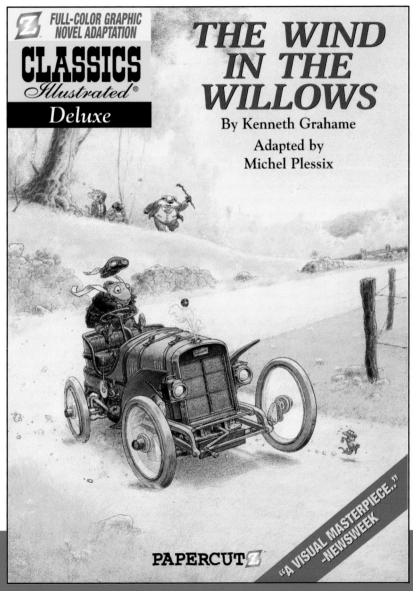

THE WIND IN THE WILLOWS

By Kenneth Grahame

Adapted by
Michel Plessix

PAPERCUTZ

"A VISUAL MASTERPIECE."
-NEWSWEEK

A Short History of
CLASSICS ILLUSTRATED...

William B. Jones Jr. is the author of Classics Illustrated: A Cultural History, which offers a comprehensive overview of the original comic-book series and the writers, artists, editors, and publishers behind-the-scenes. With Mr. Jones Jr.'s kind permission, here's a very short overview of the history of CLASSICS ILLUSTRATED adapted from his 2005 essay on Albert Kanter.

CLASSICS ILLUSTRATED was the creation of Albert Lewis Kanter, a visionary publisher, who from 1941 to 1971, introduced young readers worldwide to the realms of literature, history, folklore, mythology, and science in over 200 titles in such comicbook series as CLASSICS ILLUSTRATED and CLASSICS ILLUSTRATED JUNIOR. Kanter, inspired by the success of the first comicbooks published in the early 30s and late 40s, believed he could use the same medium to introduce young readers to the world of great literature. CLASSIC COMICS (later changed to CLASSICS ILLUSTRATED in 1947) was launched in 1941, and soon the comicbook adaptations of Shakespeare, Stevenson, Twain, Verne, and other authors, were being used in schools and endorsed by educators.

CLASSICS ILLUSTRATED was translated and distributed in countries such as Canada, Great Britain, the Netherlands, Greece, Brazil, Mexico, and Australia. The genial publisher was hailed abroad as "Papa Klassiker." By the beginning of the 1960s, CLASSICS ILLUSTRATED was the largest childrens publication in the world. The original CLASSICS ILLUSTRATED series adapted into comics 169 titles; among these were Frankenstein, 20,000 Leagues Under the Sea, Treasure Island, Julius Caesar, and Faust.

Albert L. Kanter died, March 17, 1973, leaving behind a rich legacy for the millions of readers whose imaginations were awakened by CLASSICS ILLUSTRATED.

CLASSICS ILLUSTRATED was re-launched in 1990 in graphic novel/book form by the Berkley Publishing Group and First Publishing, Inc. featuring all-new adaptations by such top graphic novelists as Rick Geary, Bill Sienkiewicz, Kyle Baker, Gahan Wilson, and others. "First had the right idea, they just came out about 15 years too soon. Now bookstores are ready for graphic novels such as these," Jim explains. Many of these excellent adaptations have been acquired by Papercutz and will make up the new series of CLASSICS ILLUSTRATED titles.

The first volume of the new CLASSICS ILLUSTRATED series presents graphic novelist Rick Geary's adaptation of "Great Expectations" by Charles Dickens. The second volume, is also by Geary, featuring his adaptation of "The Invisble Man" by H. G. Wells. The third volume, an adaptation of "Through the Looking-Glass" the follow-up to "Alice's Adventures in Wonderland" by Lewis Carroll, is by Harvey and Eisner award-winning graphic novelist Kyle Baker. The fifth features "The Raven and Other Poems" by Edgar Allan Poe and illustrated by *The New Yorker* and *Playboy* cartoonist Gahan Wilson – a sample of which appears on the following pages.

ALONE

FROM childhood's hour I have not been
As others were— I have not seen
As others saw— I could not bring
My passions from a common spring.
From the same source I have not taken
My sorrow; I could not awaken
My heart to joy at the same tone;
And all I lov'd, *I* lov'd alone.

Then— in my childhood— in the dawn
Of a most stormy life— was drawn
From ev'ry depth of good and ill
The mystery which binds me still:
From the torrent, or the fountain,
From the red cliff of the mountain,
From the sun that 'round me roll'd
In its autumn tint of gold—
From the lightning in the sky
As it pass'd me flying by—
From the thunder and the storm,
And the cloud that took the form
(When the rest of Heaven was blue)
Of a demon in my view.

Don't miss CLASSICS ILLUSTRATED #4 "The Raven and Other Poems"
by Edgar Allan Poe, illustrated by Gahan Wilson.

CAROLYN KEENE
NANCY DREW GIRL DETECTIVE®

CAROLYN KEENE
NANCY DREW
Pageant Perfect Crime

CAROLYN KEENE
NANCY DREW
Perfect Cover

CAROLYN KEENE
NANCY DREW
THE PERFECT ESCAPE

CAROLYN KEENE
NANCY DREW
SECRET IDENTITY

CAROLYN KEENE
NANCY DREW
IDENTITY THEFT

CAROLYN KEENE
NANCY DREW
IDENTITY REVEALED

Pageant Perfect Crime

Perfect Cover

Perfect Escape

Secret Identity

Identity Theft

Identity Revealed

INVESTIGATE THESE TWO THRILLING MYSTERY TRILOGIES!

Available wherever books are sold!